This book belongs to:

_____

_____

_____

To my children Ryan and Anna,

Thank you for refusing to throw away your sticky popsicle sticks because you knew you could make them into something amazing!

This story begins on a hot summer day,
when a cold tasty treat began melting away.

It was so very hot, and it happened so quick.
What once was a popsicle was now a stained stick.

Deep in a puddle that was getting quite sticky,
this sad little stick cried and felt rather icky.

Then Stick heard a voice from way up in a tree.

Please do not cry and just listen to me.
Before being a popsicle, you were part of a tree.
There's so much in this world for you to explore.
You will get through this and be more than before.

Twig quickly jumped down from the very tall tree
and said, "Stick, there is something I'd like you to see.
Sometimes things happen, and the reasons aren't clear,
but give it some time, and the answers appear."

She knew her friend Pencil could draw something grand.
Hopefully, he could help Stick understand.

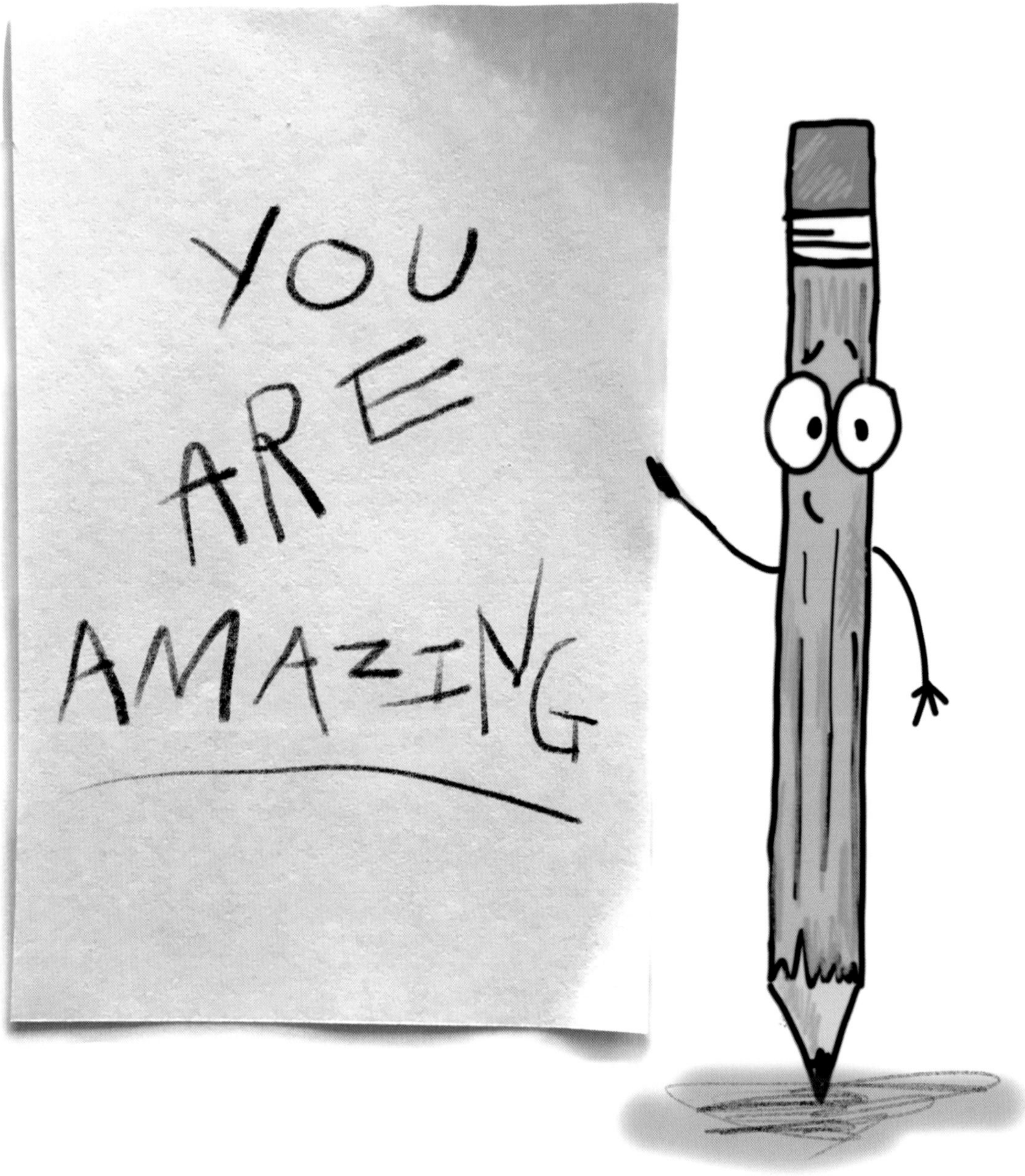
YOU
ARE
AMAZING

Can't you see? I'm just a stained stick,
my only talent was melting too quick.
I cannot draw or do a fun trick,
I'll always be just an icky, sticky stick.

Twig knew she needed to show Stick even more,
something amazing that he could not ignore.
So they went to see Brush, he was once lost too,
but now he could paint with red, yellow, and blue.

Twig saw that Stick was still very upset,
so, she thought they should go back to where they first met.
Back at the sweet puddle of sugary goo,
Twig thought Stick might find a good clue.
Then Twig looked up. "It's been there all along!
That little stick house could be where you belong."

Twig was excited. She ran up the tree

And shouted to Stick   Hurry up! Follow me!

Stick couldn't believe Twig had climbed up so high.

Just then a bluebird flew down to the ground
and lifted Stick up without making a sound.

The bird placed him gently in the last open space.
Finally Stick found his new happy place.

This is where I belong! I can make art in a tree!
It was quite a journey, **but I'm glad to be me!**

Stick never forgot that one hot summer day
and was glad that his popsicle melted away.
He made some true friends and beautiful tree art,
And learned it's never too late to have a fresh start.

Extended Learning

Show the front cover of the book again. Point to the author/illustrator name. Ask if the students know what the author and illustrator's roles are in a book. Discuss. Do they know any other names of authors and illustrators?

Who are the main characters in this book? How do the characters (specifically Stick) change throughout the book?

Discuss the main theme(s) of the book (sometimes things don't turn out the way you want, but pick yourself back up and persevere).

What are some types of sticks in the book (twig, pencil, brush, popsicle)?

What are some other things sticks can be used for in real life (canoe paddle, chair leg, chopsticks, pick up sticks game)? How do you use sticks in your life?

Give each child some popsicle sticks and have them create a project with them. Model and discuss possible ideas first (such as a raft, house, person, and rocket). Have them share their projects when they're done.

Have each child bring in some sticks from home and create a sculpture or new invention or object with them. Share their projects with the class. Discuss how something as simple as a stick became something else.

Give each child a popsicle stick to decorate. Use the group's decorated sticks to create a class project (such as a bird house). Discuss how each of us are a part of the whole.

When was a time when something bad happened to you or things didn't happen the way you wanted? How did you handle it? How could you have handled it better?

How did Twig help Stick in this book? In your life, who has helped you when you've been down? Who have you helped and how?

How to make Stick's bird house

You will need:

-Jumbo craft sticks

-Scribble stickers (sold separately, available on: www.dianealber.com)

-Hot glue (only to be used by an adult)

-Paint (watercolor paint, acrylic paint or tempra) or markers

-String (to hang the bird house)

-Clear acrylic sealer or polyurethane spray sealer (to protect from weather)

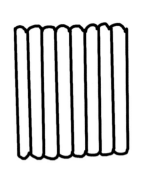

Step 1: Line up 8 jumbo craft sticks.

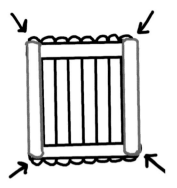

Step 2: Create a line of hot glue on top and bottom. Place a stick on both.

Step 3: Place two dots of glue on the ends and place a popsicle on top.

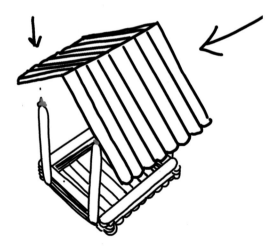

Step 4: Repeat, to build the walls of the house.

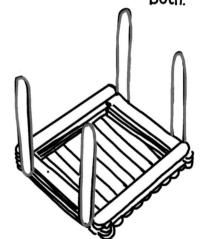

Step 5: Put hot glue on four sides to attach the posts.

GLUE

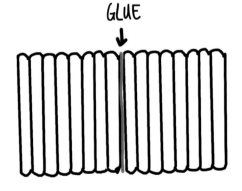

Step 6: Do steps 1 and 2 to create two panels for the roof. Glue panels together at a 90 degree angle.

Step 7: Place hot glue on the posts to secure the roof.

Step 8: Place a string under the roof to hang it! Decorate with paint or markers!

Step 9: Place scribble stickers on to decorate!

Step 10: Add sealant to protect it from weather.

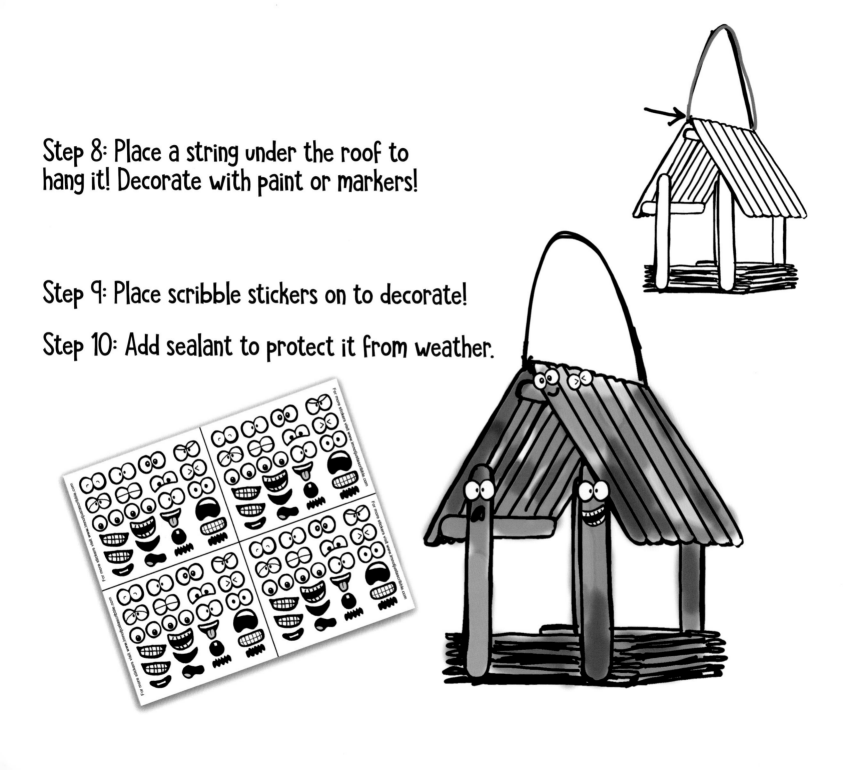